Mommy, Daddy, Me

Other books by Lyn Littlefield Hoopes

NANA

DADDY'S COMING HOME

———————

For Duncan and Sally
L. L. H.

Adam, Debbi, Gabriel
R. B.

———————

Mommy, Daddy, Me
Text copyright © 1988 by Lyn Littlefield Hoopes
Illustrations copyright © 1988 by Ruth Lercher Bornstein
Printed in the U.S.A. All rights reserved.

Library of Congress Cataloging-in-Publication Data
Hoopes, Lyn Littlefield.
    Mommy, Daddy, me.

    "A Charlotte Zolotow book."
    Summary: A little boy and his parents sail over to
visit Grandfather on a summer day.
    [1. Stories in rhyme]   I. Bornstein, Ruth Lercher, ill.
II. Title.
PZ8.3.H77Mo 1988   [E]   87-45286
ISBN 0-06-022549-1
ISBN 0-06-022550-5 (lib. bdg.)

1 2 3 4 5 6 7 8 9 10
First Edition

Lyn Littlefield Hoopes

MOMMY, DADDY, ME

pictures by Ruth Lercher Bornstein

Harper & Row, Publishers

Mommy, Daddy, me
whisper three.

Moonshine go away,
come bright day.

Come, Mommy,
come, Daddy,
kiss, us three,
Mommy, Daddy, me.

Bring in wood,
Daddy, me.

Sift, stir,
flip
flapjacks three.

Trunks and shorts,
towels and lunch,
paddles, Mommy, Daddy, me.

Pines,
beach
and sea.

A canoe for Daddy, Mommy and me.

Dip,
dip,
and glide.

Water drips
drip drops.

Fish flips
flip flops.

Still morning
seals sunning,
dip,
slip ripple
sea.

An island for Daddy, Mommy and me.

Stones and sea.
Skipping stones,
skip, Mommy and me.

Dark wood waiting still,
go high
high hill.

Mommy and Daddy.

Me.

Buttercups, come see!

An island for Daddy, Mommy and me.

Sky,
sea
and me.

Warm rocks,
wet rocks.
Daddy and Mommy,
me.

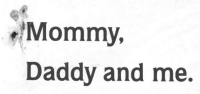

Mommy,
Daddy and me.

Daddy,
Mommy and me.

Mommy, Daddy and me.

Shine,
wind-shine sea.
Away,
us three.

Home.

Pull,
pull,
pull home.

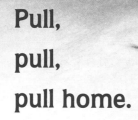

Home, Mommy, Daddy, me.

Daddy, Mommy and me.